Donatello

••••

The Radical
Robot

Other Teenage Mutant Ninja Turtles® books
available from Dell Publishing:

YEARLING BOOKS / YOUNG YEARLINGS / YEARLING CLASSICS are designed especially to entertain and enlighten young people. Patricia Reilly Giff, consultant to this series, received her bachelor's degree from Marymount College and a master's degree in history from St. John's University. She holds a Professional Diploma in Reading and a Doctorate of Humane Letters from Hofstra University. She was a teacher and reading consultant for many years, and is the author of numerous books for young readers.

For a complete listing of all Yearling titles,
write to Dell Readers Service,
P.O. Box 1045, South Holland, IL 60473.

Donatello

• • • •

The Radical Robot

• • • •

WRITTEN BY
STEPHEN MURPHY

Illustrations by
Dan Berger and Brian Thomas

A Young Yearling Book

Published by
Dell Publishing
a division of
Bantam Doubleday Dell Publishing Group, Inc.
1540 Broadway
New York, New York 10036

Licensed by Surge Licensing, Inc.

ISBN: 0-440-40860-1

Printed in the United States of America

July 1993

10 9 8 7 6 5 4 3 2 1

CWO

*To the Mirage Studios artists,
without whom there wouldn't be
any stories to tell (or sell)*

Contents

• • • •

Prologue

● ● ● ●

Our tale begins in Japan with a clan of ninja known as the Foot. The leader of the Foot was a quiet, honorable man named Hamato Yoshi.

One member of the clan sought to steal the leadership away from Hamato Yoshi. This ninja's name was Oroku Saki. He had no honor.

Through an act of treachery Saki made it look like Yoshi was planning to kill a spiritual leader who was visiting the Foot. Saki's plan was very cunning, and very evil.

Unable to offer an explanation in defense of his innocence, Yoshi was banished from the Foot clan . . . forever!

Disgraced, Yoshi fled to America. Penniless, his honor preventing him from begging or stealing, Hamato Yoshi chose to live a solitary life in the sewers beneath the city. In time Yoshi made friends with the many rats who lived there.

• • • •

One day in the city above the sewers a young boy was walking home from a pet store. He had just bought four turtles as pets and was hurrying home to show his friends.

In his haste the boy tripped. The four little turtles fell from his arms, right into a storm drain leading down to the sewers!

The boy never saw his pet turtles again.

The four turtles, however,

landed safely in the sewer water far below, directly at the feet of Hamato Yoshi! Yoshi immediately decided to care for the turtles as if they were his own. The turtles sensed Yoshi's kindness and were happy to be cared for by him.

The four turtles were brothers. They began to treat Yoshi as if he were their father.

The turtles liked their new home in the sewers. It was wet and smelly and full of interesting things. They found many places to play.

● ● ● ●

One day Hamato Yoshi found the four turtles playing in a strange, glowing ooze that had spilled from a broken cannister.

What Yoshi didn't know was that the weird ooze was *mutagen,* a substance that caused whoever touched it to take on the form of whatever creature he had most recently been in contact with!

The four turtles began to change right before Yoshi's eyes, growing, mutating, becoming more human . . . for the turtles had most recently touched Yoshi.

Yoshi had also touched the mutagen. Soon he, too, began to

mutate. But since Yoshi had most recently touched one of the many rats he had befriended, he began to take on the appearance of a rat!

Knowing that the four mutated turtles would become outcasts much like himself, Yoshi began training them in the ninja skills that he used to teach to the Foot clan back home. He dressed them each in masked costumes designed after those worn by the ninja of ancient Japan.

Yoshi then gave each turtle a name in honor of one of his favorite Renaissance painters. He also gave each of them a special weapon.

One turtle he named Leonardo. Yoshi gave Leonardo two *katana* blades.

Yoshi decided to call the second turtle Raphael. Raphael was given two *sai*s with which to defend himself.

Yoshi named the next turtle Donatello. Yoshi gave Donatello a wooden *bo* staff.

To the fourth turtle Yoshi gave a pair of whirling *nunchaku*s and the name Michaelangelo.

The turtles in turn named their rat-master Splinter. Yoshi found it very appropriate, given the fact that his newly mutated form was so different from his old one. He felt as though he had been splintered away from his old self.

Splinter liked his new name very much.

● ● ● ●

Besides training the turtles in the skills of the ninja, Yoshi began to teach them other things as well. He taught them reading, writing, and drawing. History, geography, and oceanography. Biology, zoology, and ecology. Arithmetic and geometry. Honor and respect.

As the turtles continued to learn, they each began to develop their own interests. It was not long before the four turtles were noticeably different from one another. Soon each brother had a distinctive personality all his own.

Library Visit

● ● ● ●

The four turtles and their sensei, Splinter, were walking through the city. It was night and they were all in disguise. Each of the turtles wore an overcoat and a wide-brimmed hat. Splinter wore a turtleneck sweater and a wool cap.

Michaelangelo was the first to notice that Donatello was carrying something in one of his hands.

"What's that thing?" asked Michaelangelo. He was quite puzzled.

"It's a motion detector," replied Donatello. He held it up for Michaelangelo to see.

"What does it do?" asked Splinter.

"It tells us when something nearby is moving. This way no one should be able to surprise us, or even see us," said Donatello.

Donatello liked to invent things. He liked gadgets. He

liked to know how they worked. He was very fond of taking things apart. Sometimes he put things back together differently than they were originally.

"That motion detector looks a lot like the remote control to our television," Leonardo observed.

Donatello blushed. "It is," he admitted. "I thought it would be more useful this way."

Just then the light on the motion detector flashed red.

"Someone's coming," whispered Donatello.

The turtles and Splinter hid behind some trash cans in an alley.

A woman walked by. She had a small dog on a leash. The dog wore a pink sweater. The sweater had letters written on it. The letters spelled out the dog's name. Its name was Noodles.

Raphael thought the dog looked silly. He thought its name was even sillier. Raphael did his best not to laugh out loud.

The dog wanted to sniff the trash cans, but the woman pulled it by its leash. The dog hurried along.

"They're gone now," said Donatello.

"Noodles." Raphael giggled.

The red light on the motion detector went out.

The turtles and Splinter continued along their way. They were going to the public library. Donatello had some books that were nearly overdue.

"What books are you returning?" asked Leonardo.

"Just these three," said Donatello. He held them up for Leonardo to see.

One book was entitled *Electronics for Beginners.*

Another was called *Build Your Own Computer.*

The third book was *The Age of Dinosaurs.*

Donatello liked dinosaurs. He dreamed of someday inventing a time machine that could take him back to the time of the dinosaurs. This way he could combine his two hobbies!

"We have arrived," announced Splinter. "The public library."

Donatello went over to the night depository. It was a slot on the outside wall of the library. The slot was large enough to allow a large book to fit through.

Donatello slid his three books in. He could hear them fall into a box on the inside of the library.

16

Ker-plunk, ker-chunk, ker-dunk,
went the three books.

Just then Donatello noticed
that the red light on the motion
detector was flashing!

Trouble
in Progress

● ● ● ●

The turtles and Splinter hid behind some bushes next to the library.

The red light on the motion
detector continued to flash.

Michaelangelo stuck his head
through the bushes.

He looked right and left.

He looked up and down.

He looked this way and that.

"I don't see anyone," he reported.

Splinter stuck his head through the bushes alongside Michaelangelo's.

Splinter looked straight across the street. "Look there," he said to Michaelangelo.

"Oops, I looked in every direction except straight," said Michaelangelo softly. He was embarrassed.

Across the street four boys

were crouched by the door of a store.

"Gee, it looks like those boys are about to break into that building," said Donatello. "Yo!" he yelled.

Suddenly an alarm sounded. It was coming from the building. The alarm was very loud. The four boys rushed away.

"Look!" said Raphael.

The turtles and Splinter looked.

The four boys were running toward a fifth figure. This figure looked like a man, only larger. It stood stiffly in the dark shad-

ows, directly over an open man-
hole!

Then, with a quick, machine-
like movement, it directed the
boys down into the sewers!

Into the Sewers

• • • •

Within moments the boys and the mysterious fifth figure had disappeared down the man-hole.

"Hey!" yelled Raphael.

"Hay is for horses," replied Michaelangelo.

"They're getting away!" continued Raphael. "We should do something."

"You are right, Raphael. Let us follow them and learn more," directed Splinter.

• • • •

The turtles and Splinter went into a darkened alley. Swiftly they removed their disguises.

Off came their overcoats. Off came their hats. Donatello helped Splinter take off his sweater, which was very tight.

They placed the clothes in a pile and then hid the pile behind a Dumpster.

"Gee, I wonder what those

26

boys were up to," said Raphael. "I wonder if they were really about to break into that store."

"Sure looked that way to me," said Michaelangelo.

"Otherwise, why would they have run away?" asked Leonardo.

The other turtles looked at Leonardo. He had made a good point.

"Weapons at the ready," said Splinter.

Each turtle took out his weapon.

Michaelangelo whipped out a *nunchaku*. He twirled it around several times in the night air. It made a slight breeze.

Donatello pulled out his *bo* staff. He balanced one of its ends perfectly on a finger. Then he held it firmly at its center.

Raphael held a *sai* up to the streetlight. He liked the way the light played across its polished metal surface.

Leonardo withdrew one of his *katana* blades. He held it with great respect. Its blade was very sharp.

Splinter took out his walking stick. He had taken it with him when he left Japan many years before. The stick was very hard and was a trusty weapon.

He then directed the turtles toward the open manhole.

• • • •

The turtles and Splinter entered the sewer in silence.

They paused to let their eyes adjust to the darkness within.

They gripped their weapons.

They smelled the air.

They listened very carefully.

It was very quiet within the sewer.

Too quiet.

"This is a perfect time to use my motion detector," whispered

Donatello. He reached into his belt and withdrew the small device.

The motion detector was already flashing!

"Uh-oh," said Donatello.

Just then, a large figure rushed toward them from out of the shadows!

Attack of
the Robot

● ● ● ●

"Uh-oh," repeated Donatello.

The large figure came thundering into their midst.

It was a robot!

It was blue and purple, and its eyes were solid white. It had a small symbol of a foot on its forehead but didn't have a mouth. It was big and powerful and looked very mean.

The robot spread out its muscular arms and swatted the turtles aside like they were little flies!

BOF! SHLAM! GUNCH! THUNK! went the bodies of the four turtles as they were struck by the robot.

"Aha! Here is our mysterious shadowed figure," Splinter noted, quickly avoiding the robot's move. At the same time Splinter took a closer look at the foot symbol that marked the robot's forehead. *There is some-*

thing very familiar about that symbol, he thought to himself.

"That wasn't very sporting of you," said Leonardo to the robot, getting to his feet. "In fact I think it was very rude."

Leonardo leapt at the robot. He had both of his *katana* blades out, one in each hand.

Ka-tang! Ka-tang! went the blades, striking the robot's shoulders. But the *katana*s bounced right off the robot. They didn't make a scratch. Not even a dent.

"My turn!" yelled Michaelangelo. He made a tough-looking face at the robot.

35

Michaelangelo held a *nun-chaku* in each hand. He whirled and twirled first one, then the other. Then he whirled and twirled them together.

It was very impressive.

The robot looked at the *nun-chaku*s. It seemed puzzled. Sensing its confusion, Michaelangelo leapt at the robot.

Whappity - whappity - whap! went the *nunchaku*s, striking the robot on both sides of its head. But the *nunchaku*s bounced right off the robot.

They didn't make a scratch. Not even a dent.

"I guess I'll have to handle

this," said Raphael. With that he jumped onto the robot's shoulders.

He used both his *sai*s like two jackhammers. He brought them down repeatedly on top of the robot's head.

Chik-chik-chik-chik-chik-chik-chik! went the *sai*s, right at the center of the robot's head.

One *sai* made a little scratch. The other made a small dent.

The robot didn't like this. He picked Raphael off his shoulders and flung him into Splinter.

"Sorry, master," said Raphael.

"Your foot is on my tail," replied Splinter.

Donatello faced the robot. He placed his *bo* staff down upon the ground.

The robot looked down at Donatello. If it had had a mouth, it would have smiled an evil smile.

The robot advanced toward Donatello.

"I sure hope you know what you're doing, Donatello," called Leonardo.

"So do I," replied Donatello.

The robot towered over him. It flexed its muscular arms. It began to curl its powerful hands into fists.

Donatello ducked and ran straight between the robot's legs.

Then he climbed up its back before the robot could turn around to grab him.

"What are you doing?" asked Michaelangelo.

"I'm looking for something that I read about in one of my library books," answered Donatello.

Michaelangelo thought about it. He knew it couldn't have been the book about dinosaurs. Maybe the book about computers? Possibly. Or maybe the book on electronics.

"The book on electronics?" asked Michaelangelo.

The robot was reaching back for Donatello.

Donatello clung to the robot's back. Its arms couldn't bend to reach Donatello.

"That's right, Mikie," said Donatello.

"I read that many electronic gadgets have '*kill* switches' hidden on them." He squinted at the back of the robot's head.

"What's a kill switch?" asked Michaelangelo.

Donatello smiled. He jabbed a finger at a spot on the back of the robot's head.

The robot fell to the floor.

"A kill switch is like an emergency *off* button," he answered.

Donatello stood proudly over the fallen robot. "I simply shut the robot off." He beamed.

The turtles and Splinter stood around the fallen robot.

Raphael kicked at one of its arms. Leonardo poked at one of its legs.

"Well done, my son," Splinter said to Donatello.

"Thanks, master," said Donatello.

Donatello looked down at the robot. Its design impressed him. "Um, master?" asked Donatello. "Can I take him home?"

Splinter and the other turtles stared at Donatello in amazement.

"Why do you want to take the robot home?" asked Splinter, clearly puzzled by Donatello's question.

"So that I can see how it works," Donatello replied.

"Maybe the robot can provide us clues to what those boys were up to, or even to where they went," said Leonardo.

"Right," said Donatello. "And maybe we can even learn who built the robot!"

Splinter looked down at the fallen robot. His gaze lingered

for a moment on the foot symbol that marked the robot's fore-head. Then Splinter turned to Donatello.

"All right," said Splinter.

Donatello smiled.

New Attitude

• • • •

Donatello was up late. His brothers and Splinter had all gone to sleep several hours ago. But Donatello stayed up to work on his new robot.

He had discovered that the back of the robot's head was a panel. The panel was like a small door. It opened to reveal a programming pad. There were buttons with the alphabet written on them. There were buttons with symbols. There were several small circuit boards.

Don was determined to learn how to reprogram the robot.

He thought long and deep.

He tinkered and he fiddled.

He thought and he thought.

He made a cup of hot chocolate.

He stayed up very, very late.

Too Cool

● ● ● ●

In the morning Splinter found
Donatello asleep on the couch.

Splinter went about his morning routine. He decided not to
wake Donatello. He didn't bother
to wake the other turtles, either,
asleep in their bunk beds. He

knew they needed their rest after yesterday's battle.

Splinter went to the kitchen. He wanted to make himself his usual morning cup of ginseng tea.

In the kitchen Splinter met up with a big surprise.

The robot was making Splinter's tea! It had placed a tea bag in a cup and set the cup upon the kitchen table. The robot had placed a spoon next to the cup and had taken the jar of honey out of the cupboard. It was in the process of boiling some water on the kitchen stove.

The robot was wearing an

apron. It turned to look at Splinter. If it had a mouth, it would have smiled the friendliest of smiles.

"Donatello!" shouted Splinter.

● ● ● ●

Donatello awoke from a dream.

The dream had been about dinosaurs that rode motorcycles. Donatello had been helping a tyrannosaurus change a flat tire.

"Donatello!" shouted Splinter a second time.

Donatello ran into the kitchen. So did his three brothers, who had been awakened by Splinter's shouts.

"What's wrong, master?" asked Donatello.

"Breakfast appears to be served," responded Splinter.

The turtles looked at the kitchen table. The table was covered with dishes of food.

There were pancakes and waffles and three types of syrup. There were two types of toast and five brands of cereal. There was a selection of cooked eggs and a choice of bacon or sausage. Also whole milk and skim milk, in both regular and chocolate. A big bowl of fresh fruit and some porridge with cinnamon on it was in the center of the table.

"Who prepared all this?" asked Leonardo.

"He did," answered Splinter, pointing to the robot.

The robot was busy baking fresh doughnuts.

Donatello smiled.

● ● ● ●

After breakfast the turtles napped.

Michaelangelo was the first to wake up. He had fallen asleep on the kitchen floor with a jelly doughnut in his right hand. He finished eating the doughnut, then rolled over on his side and looked into the living room.

His brothers were still asleep.

Splinter sat in his favorite chair, meditating. The robot was brushing Splinter's fur!

Michaelangelo stared at the robot. He had an idea.

● ● ● ●

Later, when everyone was awake, the turtles exercised.

Then it was time for their ninja training. Splinter noticed how slowly the turtles were moving during the lessons. Must be the big breakfast they had had earlier, he concluded.

After training, Michaelangelo told his brothers his idea.

Everyone agreed that it was a good one.

With Donatello's help Michaelangelo put his plan into action.

• • • •

It was time for supper.

"Excellent idea, Michaelangelo," said Raphael.

"Thanks!" replied Michaelangelo.

The turtles and Splinter sat around the kitchen table. The robot was standing by the counter. It was opening six boxes of six different brands of pizza.

Michaelangelo had sent the robot out for pizza. The robot had gone all over the city buying the best pizzas in town. It had even bought a big chunk of cheese for Splinter.

The turtles ate all the pizzas, even the crust.

● ● ● ●

Soon they were sleepy.

"If you must nap, please sleep in your beds and not on the kitchen floor," said Splinter.

The turtles went to their bedroom. They shared the same

room and had two double bunk beds.

Michaelangelo and Raphael had the top bunks. Donatello and Leonardo had the bottom bunks.

"I just thought of something," said Donatello.

"What's that?" asked Leonardo.

"The robot doesn't have a name," said Donatello.

"I know what we can call him," said Raphael.

"What's that?" asked Donatello.

Raphael giggled. "Noodles," he said.

Mystery Figure

• • • •

The four boys were in trouble.
They had lost one of their
leader's robots. And now they
were facing their leader.

"What happened?!" the leader
yelled. He was a very mysterious
figure, who always sat in the

deep shadows of his headquarters.

The leader wore a mask. The boys had never seen his face. He was always angry and liked to yell. The boys were afraid of him.

"Well?" continued the leader. "What happened to my robot?!"

"We . . . we were being followed," said one of the boys.

"Yeah," said another. "We tried to break into that store the way you wanted, but then we were scared away."

"Scared away? By who?!" demanded the leader. He was growing angry at the boys.

"We don't know. We kept going. The robot stayed behind to fight," said the first boy.

"It isn't our fault," said one of the other boys.

"Fools," said the leader.

The leader stared at them for a long time. Then he reached into his cape and pulled out a small device. He held it in one of his hands. The device looked a lot like the remote control to a television. Except it had one big button.

"What's that thing?" asked the first boy.

"It's a homing beacon and override switch," growled the leader. "It sends out a signal

that orders the robot home. It also overrides any reprogramming that may have been done to the robot," he said with a smirk.

He pressed the button.

Bad Attitude

• • • •

The robot was busy sweeping up in the kitchen.

The turtles had made quite a mess eating their supper. There were anchovies under the table and pepperoni slices on the chairs. Not to mention all the crumbs that were everywhere.

The robot hurried. Donatello had programmed it to clean the bathroom once it had finished in the kitchen.

Suddenly the robot stopped.

There was a flash of light deep within its eyes. The robot stiffened. It looked at the broom in its hands and at the apron that it was wearing. If it had had a mouth, it would have smiled a very nasty smile.

The robot lifted one of its feet and squashed an anchovy beneath its heavy boot.

The homing beacon had found its mark.

"Donatello!" shouted Splinter.

Donatello awoke from a dream. His dream had been about dinosaurs that roamed the cities of an alien world. Donatello was a scientist who was trying to herd the dinosaurs into a huge spaceship. An asteroid was about to collide with the dinosaurs' world. The impact would send tons of dust into the planet's atmosphere, blocking out all sunlight. Within months the planet would be too cold for the dinosaurs to live upon. It was up to Donatello to save the dinosaurs from certain extinction.

"Donatello!" shouted Splinter a second time.

Donatello woke up and ran into the living room with his brothers.

"Your help would be most welcome," said Splinter. He and the robot were fighting. It looked as though they were fencing with swords. But neither of them had a sword. Splinter held his walking stick. He was trying to hit the robot with it.

The robot held up the broom. He was trying to hit Splinter with it.

The walking stick and the broom smashed against each

other. This happened many times.

It looked exactly like Splinter and the robot were fencing, thought Donatello. But then this would mean that the robot had somehow turned *bad* again, he realized.

"Weapons at the ready," commanded Splinter.

The turtles joined Splinter in battle against the rampaging robot.

Final Battle

● ● ● ●

"I wish Noodles would take off that apron," said Raphael. He giggled. He had a hard time taking the fight seriously with the robot dressed up in that outfit.

The robot struck Raphael with the broom. Raphael stopped gig-

71

gling. "Hey, this is serious," he said.

"Most serious," said Splinter.

Donatello did not understand what had gone wrong. The robot should not be fighting. It should have been cleaning the bathroom.

Something had gone wrong with the robot's reprogramming, Donatello realized.

Just then the robot kicked over Splinter's favorite chair. Then it tipped over the coffee table. And knocked over the bookcase.

Books spilled all over the floor. The robot picked up the turtles' favorite book on Bruce Lee and hit Leonardo over the head with it.

Time to act, thought Donatello. He used his *bo* staff as a pole vault.

Donatello flew through the air and landed on the robot's back. He jabbed his fingers at the kill switch on the back of the robot's neck. *This will shut off the robot,* thought Donatello.

It didn't.

The robot threw Donatello into a lamp.

It knocked Raphael and Michaelangelo's heads together. *Konk!* went their heads.

The robot lifted one of its heavy boots and brought it down on Splinter's tail.

Splinter squealed. He turned to Donatello. "This robot has to go," he said.

The robot picked up a big box of the turtles' comic books. The box was old and weak, and its bottom gave out. Comics spilled everywhere. Many of the pages folded. Several covers came off completely.

Donatello knew that Splinter was right. The robot had to go. And Donatello knew that it was his responsibility to get rid of the robot. It had been his idea to bring the robot home.

What could he do, though? he wondered.

The robot lunged toward Donatello's computer. Donatello had built the computer himself. He had learned how to build it from reading a library book. He was proud of his computer. It had taken a lot of work to assemble.

The robot began to pick up the computer.

Donatello leapt into action. He struck the robot with his *bo* staff.

It was a mighty blow. Donatello had never struck anything with such force before.

The robot fell to the floor with a mighty crash.

It was very still.

Donatello knelt down by the fallen robot. He could hear circuits popping within the robot's head. He heard some whirring sounds and other noises that didn't sound right. Then Donatello saw a light flash on and off behind the robot's eyes.

The robot made no more sounds. It lay very still.

The battle was over.

The turtles and Splinter were triumphant.

Questions

● ● ● ●

"So."

It was Splinter. He was sitting in his favorite chair. He was thinking.

The turtles were on the floor. They were going through their comic-book collection. And they weren't happy.

Donatello looked up at Splinter. He held a copy of *Mega Dino Corps* in his right hand. In his left hand he held its cover. It was one of his favorite comic books.

"Yes, master?" asked Donatello.

Splinter addressed Donatello. "Why do you think the robot turned against us?" he asked.

Donatello had given this a lot of thought. "I think someone reprogrammed my reprogramming," he answered.

"But no one could have come in here without our knowing it," said Leonardo. He was trying to unfold a crease in the cover of *Samurai from Saturn.*

"I think someone repro-grammed the robot using a re-mote control," said Donatello. "He did it from far away, from wherever the robot came from," he added. "It's the only solution I can come up with," he concluded.

Splinter thought about this. He leaned back in his chair and curled his tail into a circle.

He agreed with Donatello. Splinter knew that whoever built the robot was a powerful and evil person.

Splinter looked at his adopted sons. He knew that they had

much more training to undergo before being ready to battle such a powerful villain. Then he crawled down and helped the turtles sort out their comic-book collection.

• • • •

Later Splinter made hot chocolate for everyone. He decided it was time to tell them what he suspected was the meaning of the foot symbol that was marked on the robot's forehead.

"My sons," Splinter began, "did you notice anything strange about the robot's appearance?"

"It didn't have a mouth," Michaelangelo answered.

"Yes, but besides that," said Splinter.

"It was blue and purple, and its eyes were solid white," Raphael replied.

"Yes, but was there anything else?" asked Splinter.

"There was a symbol of a foot on its forehead," said Leonardo.

"Correct," said Splinter. "The symbol of the foot. What importance does this symbol have in our lives, especially in my own?"

"The . . . the ninja clan that you belonged to in Japan was

called the Foot!" Donatello exclaimed.

"Precisely," said Splinter. "I fear that the Foot clan may be responsible for the robot, as well as for the boys who tried to break into that store near the library."

"I don't understand, master," said Michaelangelo. "I thought the Foot clan was a *good* clan."

"It was, under *my* leadership," replied Splinter. "But perhaps not so under the leadership of the man who stole the leadership from me, the evil and dishonorable Oroku Saki."

"Gee," said Leonardo, "if Saki's behind the robot, then maybe he's here in America and he's up to no good."

"Perhaps so," said Splinter. "That is why we must pay close attention to our surroundings at all times and also why you four must work very hard at your ninja training."

● ● ● ●

Later that evening Splinter allowed the four turtles to take a short walk up the sewer tunnel that led from their home. He could tell that they wanted an opportunity to talk among themselves.

"Wow, what if Oroku Saki

really is in America and created that robot? What are we going to do if we run into him?" asked Michaelangelo, a little worried.

"We'll kick his shell," replied Raphael. "Just like we did to Noodles." He giggled. Then he kicked at an old soda can and sent it flying down the sewer tunnel.

"I bet we'll have to use all of our ninja training," said Leonardo.

"And all of our knowledge, especially if Saki has more robots at his command," said Donatello.

"No problem," said Raphael, pointing at his two *sai*s.

"You're right!" Michaelangelo exclaimed. "With our combined ninja skills and our four-gazillion brain cells, we're ready for anything!"

With that said, they slapped each other's palms and together yelled, "Cowabunga!"

Then they headed back inside to begin taping up their damaged comic books.